CAPTAIN AMERICA™

WINTER SOLDIER

Reader Services

CUSTOMER SERVICE IN THE UK AND REPUBLIC OF IRELAND
How to continue your collection:
Customers can either place an order with their newsagent or receive issues on subscription.
Back issues: Either order through your newsagent or write to: Marvel Collection, Jacklin Enterprises UK, PO Box 77, Jarrow, NE32 3YII, enclosing payment of the cover price plus £1.00 p&p per copy. (Republic of Ireland: cover price plus €1.75). Subscriptions: You can have your issues sent directly to your home. For details, see insert in issue 1 or phone our Customer Service Hotline on 0871 472 4240 (Monday to Friday, 9am-5pm, calls cost 10p per minute from UK landline). Alternatively you can write to Marvel Collection, Jacklin Enterprises UK, PO Box 77, Jarrow, NE32 3YH, or fax your enquiries to 0871 472 4241, or e-mail: marvelcollection@jacklinservice.com or visit www.graphicnovelcollection.com

CUSTOMER SERVICE IN OVERSEAS MARKETS

Australia: Back issues can be ordered from your newsagent. Alternatively telephone (03) 9872 4000 or write to: Back Issues Department, Bissett Magazine Services, PO Box 3460, Nunawading Vic 3131. Please enclose payment of the cover price, plus A$2.49 (inc. GST) per issue postage and handling. Back issues are subject to availability.
Subscriptions: You can have your issues sent directly to your home. For details, see insert in issue 1 or phone our Customer Service Hotline on (03) 9872 4000. Alternatively you can write to Hachette subs offer, Bissett Magazine Services, PO Box 3460, Nunawading Vic 3131, or fax your enquiries to (03) 9873 4988, or order online at www.bissettmags.com.au

New Zealand: For back issues, ask your local magazine retailer or write to: Netlink, PO Box 47906, Ponsonby, Auckland.
South Africa: Back issues are available through your local CNA store or other newsagent.
Subscriptions: call (011) 265 4309, fax (011) 314 2984, or write to: Marvel Collection, Private Bag 10, Centurion 0046 or e-mail: service@jacklin.co.za
Malta: Back issues are only available through your local newsagent
Malaysia: Call (03) 8023 3260, or e-mail: sales@allscript.com
Singapore: Call (65) 287 7090, or e-mail: sales@allscript.com

Published by Hachette Partworks Ltd, Jordan House, 47 Brunswick Place, London, N1 6EB
www.hachettepartworks.co.uk

Distributed in the UK and Republic of Ireland by Marketforce

This special edition published in 2012 by Hachette Partworks Ltd. forming part of The Ultimate Marvel Graphic Novel Collection.

Printed in China.
ISBN: 978-1-906965-93-8

Licensed by Marvel Characters B.V. through Panini S.p.A., Italy. All Rights Reserved.

CAPTAIN AMERICA™

ED BRUBAKER
WRITER

STEVE EPTING
MICHAEL LARK (ISSUE #9 AND ISSUE #12 FLASHBACK ART)
PENCILS

STEVE EPTING & MIKE PERKINS
MICHAEL LARK (ISSUE #9 AND ISSUE #12 FLASHBACK ART)
FINISHES

FRANK D'ARMATA
COLOURS

VIRTUAL CALLIGRAPHY'S CHRIS ELIOPOULOS,
RANDY GENTILE & JOE CARAMAGNA
LETTERS

TOM BREVOORT
EDITOR

MOLLY LAZER & AUBREY SITTERSON
ASSISTANT EDITORS

ANDY SCHMIDT
ASSOCIATE EDITOR

JOE QUESADA
EDITOR IN CHIEF

CAPTAIN AMERICA CREATED BY **JOE SIMON** & **JACK KIRBY**

Captain America: Winter Soldier

Marco M. Lupoi
Panini Publishing Director (Europe)

It's fair to say that the early 2000s were a difficult time to be writing Captain America. With the US still reeling from the 9/11 attacks and an administration that was growingly controversial, a hero emblazoned in the stars and stripes was never going to be an easy sell. Which America did he stand for? The left wing calling for the President's impeachment or the right wing demanding that America's military might bring swift, decisive justice upon its enemies?

Wisely, writer Ed Brubaker, stayed well away from any real world analogies and instead began to craft a story inspired by one of the key events in Cap's life - the death of his best friend and wartime sidekick Bucky. But when the first rumours began to surface about Brubaker's intentions for the character there was a fair deal of outrage. Bucky... resurrected?! Many fans considered James Buchannan Barnes demise intrinsic to Cap's back-story. His death, like Peter Parker's Uncle Ben, was sacrosanct, never to be undone at risk of diminishing the character.

However, Brubaker ignored the protests and, along with artist Steve Epting, created a tale that blew fans away. The naysayers were silenced and pretty much all of comic fandom agreed that Brubaker had achieved the impossible. Not only had he found a credible way to bring Bucky back that enriched Captain America's world, he also made the title a must-have comic once again.

So, read on, to discover the secret history of the Winter Soldier...

ontains material originally published in magazine form as CAPTAIN AMERICA VOL. 5 #8-9 & 11-14. Senior Editor (Hachette Partworks Ltd.), Sarah Gale. Packaged by Panini Publishing, a
vision of Panini UK Limited. Mike Riddell, Managing Director. Alan O'Keefe, Managing Editor. Ed Hammond, Editor. Marco M. Lupoi, Publishing Director Europe.
m Warran-Smith, Designer. Additional content: Rich Johnson. Office of publication: Brockbourne House, 77 Mount Ephraim, Tunbridge Wells, Kent TN4 8BS. No similarity between any
f the names, characters, persons and/or institutions in this edition with those of any living or dead person or institution is intended, and any such similarity which may exist is purely
oincidental. This publication may not be sold, except by authorised dealers, and is sold subject to the condition that it shall not be sold or distributed with any part of its cover or marking
moved, nor in a mutilated condition.

THE STORY SO FAR...

Events leading up to Captain America: Winter Soldier

The Red Skull, Captain America's fascist archenemy, plans to detonate Weapons of Mass Destruction in a number of American cities. However, before he can go through with his diabolical plan, he is shot dead by an unknown cybernetic assassin, working under the orders of rogue Soviet General Aleksander Lukin.

When the global espionage agency SHIELD investigate the crime scene, they discover that the Red skull was in possession of a slightly damaged Cosmic Cube, an immensely powerful device capable of warping reality itself.

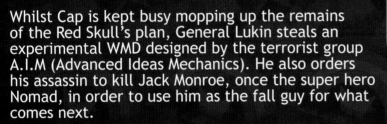

Whilst Cap is kept busy mopping up the remains of the Red Skull's plan, General Lukin steals an experimental WMD designed by the terrorist group A.I.M (Advanced Ideas Mechanics). He also orders his assassin to kill Jack Monroe, once the super hero Nomad, in order to use him as the fall guy for what comes next.

Cap arrives in Philadelphia to rescue his one-time love, SHIELD Agent Sharon Carter. Whilst there, Sharon reveals that she suspects Lukin's mysterious assassin is none other than Bucky, Cap's old World War 2 partner who seemingly died in 1945. Suddenly, the city is rocked by an explosion as the WMD Lukin stole from A.I.M. is detonated. Many innocent people are killed, allowing the Soviet General to somehow use their pain and suffering to repair and re-power the Cosmic Cube in his possession...

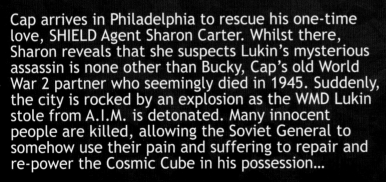

PRESENT DAY.

I'M SORRY, WHAT AM I SUPPOSED TO BE *LOOKING* AT HERE, FURY?

I THINK YOU CAN FIGURE IT OUT, ROGERS. JUST *LOOK*.

I ALREADY *TOLD* HIM, NICK. HE'S *NOT* GOING TO LISTEN...

SO, YOU EXPECT ME TO BELIEVE, *WHAT*...THAT THESE ARE PICTURES OF *BUCKY*?

THEN SHARON'S RIGHT...I'M *NOT* GOING TO LISTEN TO THAT.

STEVE. I *SAW* HIM, CLOSE-UP. *YOU--*

IT'S A TRICK.

ISN'T THAT WHAT YOU SAID WHEN THE *RED SKULL* WAS KILLED?

NO...THIS IS *DIFFERENT...* THIS--

YOU EXPECT ME TO *BELIEVE* THAT BUCKY IS STILL *ALIVE*...THAT HE'S WORKING FOR THE ENEMY...

...THAT *HE'S* RESPONSIBLE FOR WHAT HAPPENED IN *PHILADELPHIA* LAST NIGHT?

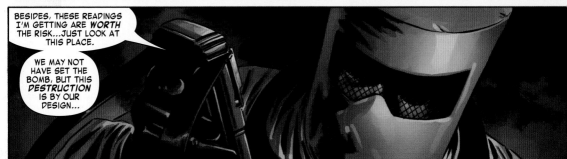

THESE ARE SURVEILLANCE PHOTOS TAKEN NEAR AIRPORTS, TRAIN STATIONS, AND BORDER CROSSINGS...AND THEY'RE *NOT* RECENT PICTURES.

THIS ONE IS FROM WEST BERLIN, IN 1955, SAME NIGHT GENERAL KELLER HAD HIS BRAINS BLOWN OUT.

THIS IS LONDON, 1960...THE MORNING AFTER THE TOP MAN AT MI6 WAS FOUND DROWNED IN HIS BATHTUB.

THIS IS SWITZERLAND, 1976. SAME DAY THAT THE VICE-CHANCELLOR OF WAKANDA FELL OFF A MOUNTAIN.

HE WAS THERE FOR A GLOBAL ECONOMIC SUMMIT, AS WELL AS THE SKIING.

THE POINT IS, THESE ARE PEOPLE ARRIVING OR LEAVING AROUND THE TIMES OF ASSASSINATIONS THAT HAD *MAJOR IMPACT* ON THE COLD WAR.

AND IN ALL OF THEM, WE'VE BEEN ABLE TO ISOLATE *THIS MAN*... AND THE FINEST FACIAL RECOGNITION SOFTWARE IN THE WORLD TELLS ME THAT IT'S THE SAME GUY.

YET *NONE* OF YOUR PREDECESSORS *EVER* NOTICED THIS?

WE'RE TALKING THOUSANDS OF CROWD PHOTOS TO LOOK THROUGH, AND THE GUY IS *GOOD*. HE'S A PROFILE HERE OR THERE, MOSTLY.

AND THIS WAS THE OLD DAYS. THE *TECH* WASN'T THERE YET, NOT FOR STUFF *LIKE THIS*.

THERE'S SOMETHING *ELSE*, TOO, THAT OUR 21ST CENTURY SOFTWARE IS ABLE TO TELL US...

BETWEEN 1955 AND 1976 IT'S ESTIMATED OUR HITTER ONLY AGED APPROXIMATELY *FIVE* YEARS.

HOW IS THAT POSSIBLE?

WELL, YOU AND I KNOW A FEW WAYS BETWEEN US...BUT THIS ONE...

BEST GUESS IS BECAUSE HE'S A COLD WAR MYTH THAT'S TURNIN' OUT TO BE TRUE.

WHAT MYTH?

THEY CALLED HIM THE *WINTER* SOLDIER.

SUPPOSED TO BE THE KGB'S SECRET WEAPON. A GUY WHO COULD PASS FOR AMERICAN AND SLIP BEHIND ENEMY LINES OR CROSS BORDERS WITHOUT RAISIN' AN EYEBROW.

DEADLY WITH A KNIFE OR A RIFLE...EVEN *DEADLIER* HAND-TO-HAND.

AND SINCE HE WAS A GHOST, HALF THE TIME THEY WEREN'T EVEN SURE IF IT WAS AN ACCIDENT OR A MURDER.

STORY WENT THAT THEY KEPT HIM *ON ICE* AND ONLY WOKE HIM UP FOR THE BIG GIGS. HE'D BE IN *STASIS* FOR FIVE YEARS...THEN OUT IN THE WORLD FOR SIX MONTHS WORKING...

...AND BACK TO RIP VAN WINKLE-LAND ONCE THE *BODIES* HIT THE MORGUE.

BUT LIKE I SAID, UNTIL TODAY, THE WINTER SOLDIER WAS A *MYTH.*

SOMEONE FOR THE SUITS TO HANG SUSPICIOUS DEATHS ON, BUT FAR AS I CAN TELL, NO ONE EVER REALLY *BELIEVED* HE EXISTED.

BUT I DO, BECAUSE I'VE GOT THIS PICTURE FROM LAST WEEK AT DULLES INTERNATIONAL... HERE HE IS *AGAIN,* ABOUT THREE YEARS OLDER THAN HE WAS IN '76...

...AND LEAVING THE BAGGAGE TURNSTILES WHERE WE LATER FOUND THE WEAPON THAT KILLED THE RED SKULL.

NICK...TAKE A STEP BACK HERE. WHAT ARE YOU SAYING?

YOU CAN'T *SERIOUSLY* BE IMPLYING THAT THIS WINTER SOLDIER PERSON IS *BUCKY?*

WHY DON'T YOU TELL ME? YOU'RE THE ONE WHO SAW HIM LAST NIGHT...

HIVE MIND...
WONDERFUL.

SMAK

KNCH

UNNH!

KRAK!

BUCKY...?

WHO THE HELL IS BUCKY?

STEVE...?

SO, WHAT'S THE PLAN, NICK? I KNOW YOU *MUST* HAVE ONE.

I DO. WE'VE GOT A *PRIME SUSPECT* IN THE TERROR ATTACK ON PHILADELPHIA... ALEKSANDER LUKIN.

AND UNFORTUNATELY, IF HE *IS* OUR MAN, HE ALSO HAS A *FULLY-CHARGED* COSMIC CUBE NOW. SO WE'RE GOING TO HAVE TO MOVE FAST.

SMALL TEAM, IN AND OUT, GRAB LUKIN AND GET HIM BACK HERE FOR QUESTIONING BEFORE THEY EVEN KNOW HE'S GONE...

...AND IF WE HAPPEN TO STUMBLE ACROSS ANYONE *ELSE*...WE'LL JUST CROSS THAT BRIDGE, Y'KNOW...?

I'M IN.

I KNOW.

I'M *WORRIED* ABOUT HIM. LAST NIGHT REALLY TOOK A TOLL...HE'S BLAMING *HIMSELF*...

THEY MANIPULATED HIM RIGHT TO A FRONT ROW SEAT FOR THIS-- THIS--

TAKE A WALK WITH ME, AGENT 13.

SIR?

WALK WITH ME.

NICK, WHAT THE *HELL?* WHAT'S GOING ON?

IT'S AGENT TAPPER.

IT'S *OVER* BETWEEN ME AND NEAL. WHAT'S *THAT* GOT--

NO...HE WAS THE ONE WHO FOUND THE BOMB LAST NIGHT...

...HE'S *DEAD,* SHARON. NEAL'S DEAD.

JUST OUTSIDE RENO, NEVADA

--NO, I DON'T THINK SO. I MEAN, FOR ONE THING, WHO'D WANNA *DATE* THE FREAKIN' *HULK?*

PEOPLE WANTED TO DATE TED BUNDY.

BUT AT LEAST *HE* WAS *HUMAN...* OR, YOU KNOW, HUMA*NOID.* NO, I'M TELLING YOU...

OKAY, SO *MAYBE* YOU'D BE SHORT OF CHICKS, BUT JUST THINK ABOUT THE *STEAM* YOU COULD BLOW OFF...

BOSS TICKS YOU OFF, YOU TOSS HIS HOUSE AT THE *SUN.* THAT KINDA RAGE AND--

HOLD ON.

WHAT?

WHERE'S MURPHY? WASN'T HE ON *SENTRY?*

S'POSED TO BE.

HANG ON, I'M GONNA CALL THIS IN.

PATROL TWELVE TO CONTROL. WE'VE GOT AN EMPTY--

HRRRUUKK!

RONNIE!

ETA IN NINETY MINUTES, COLONEL FURY.

GOOD. ANY SIGN OF *TROUBLE?*

NO SIR, ALL CLEAR SO FAR.

WHAT?

NOTHING.

IT'S *NEVER* NOTHING WITH *YOU.* WHAT IS IT? SPEAK.

WE'RE HEADING INTO A FIREFIGHT, SHARON. *MAYBE* A BIG ONE.

AND I DON'T WANT US GOING INTO IT WITH OUR *OWN* BAGGAGE, TOO.

YEAH? WELL, *YOU* SHOULD HAVE THOUGHT OF THAT EARLIER, THEN, SHOULDN'T YOU?

HEY!

OH, HEY SHARON...

WHAT THE HELL DO YOU THINK YOU'RE *DOING*, YOU SON OF A %@#$&?!

WELL, I JUST *FINISHED* A TWENTY MILE RUN, AND I WAS *PLANNING* TO WORK ON THE HEAVY BAG FOR A WHILE...

DON'T TRY AND GET *CUTE* WITH THIS, *STEVE ROGERS!*

YOU TOLD FURY TO TAKE ME *OFF THE TEAM* FOR THE KRONAS OP.

DANGER HIGH VOLTAGE

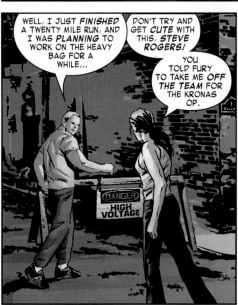

HE *TOLD* YOU?

NO, *YOU* DID...JUST *NOW.*

LIKE NICK FURY'S GOING TO GIVE YOU UP.

WHY DON'T WE TAKE THIS INSIDE?

JUST TELL ME WHAT YOU'RE *THINKING.* I'M ONE OF THE BEST *FIELD AGENTS* THEY'VE GOT.

IDENTITY-- STEVE ROGERS. ACCESS GRANTED.

SURE YOU ARE, BUT YOU'RE *TOO CLOSE* TO THIS ONE.

OH, AND YOU'RE *NOT?*

NOT THE WAY YOU ARE.

I WANT *JUSTICE* FOR THOSE PEOPLE WHO DIED IN PHILADELPHIA, AND I WANT *ANSWERS...*

...YOU'RE LOOKING FOR *REVENGE.*

OH, YOU ARE *SO FULL* OF IT! YOU DON'T THINK I CAN *TELL* WHEN YOU'RE KEEPING YOUR ANGER *BOTTLED UP?*

JUST ADMIT THAT YOU DON'T WANT ME ALONG BECAUSE YOU'RE *SCARED...*

OF *WHAT?*

THAT I'LL *KILL* HIM... BUCKY.

ANY REASON WE'RE NOT MEETING ON THE HELICARRIER, NICK?

YEAH, A DAMN GOOD ONE.

CARE TO TELL ME?

NOT REALLY... BUT I WILL.

I CAN'T GET CLEARANCE FOR THE OP.

THEY TURNED YOU DOWN?

I DIDN'T EVEN ASK, BECAUSE WHAT WE'VE GOT IS SO SLIM, THERE'S JUST NO WAY.

THE MAN IS A MASS-MURDERER. A TERRORIST. HOW CAN--

THE MAN IS SMART, TOO. HE DID JUST ENOUGH SO WE'D KNOW IT WAS HIM...

...BUT LEFT US NO WAY TO PROVE IT.

HELL, HIS HANDS ARE SO CLEAN IT'S DISGUSTING... ACCORDING TO THE EVIDENCE, *JACK MONROE* IS THE PRIME SUSPECT IN BOTH THE MURDER OF THE RED SKULL *AND* THE BOMBING IN PHILLY.

JACK...

ANOTHER THING THIS LUKIN HAS TAKEN FROM ME.

ANYWAY, WE'RE GOING IN REGARDLESS. BUT IT'S GONNA BE TRICKY.

WHEN LUKIN DISAPPEARED OFF THE MAP IN RUSSIA, IT TURNS OUT HIS FIRST MOVE WAS TO PURCHASE LAND FROM CHINA, ALONG THE MONGOLIAN BORDER.

THE LEGALITY OF THIS IS SHAKY, BUT THAT PIECE OF LAND IS THE *HEADQUARTERS* OF KRONAS INTERNATIONAL. IT'S A CORPORATE-OWNED COUNTRY, BASICALLY.

LIKE HE STARTED HIS OWN LITTLE EMPIRE.

AND WE'RE GOING TO TOPPLE IT?

IN TWO DAYS. OUR INTEL SAYS LUKIN AND THE MEMBERS OF THE BOARD ARE HAVIN' A POWWOW ABOUT THEIR NEW MERGER WITH ROXXON. SO THEY'LL ALL BE THERE...

THAT WORKS FOR ME... BUT...

WHAT?

WE NEED TO TALK ABOUT AGENT 13'S INVOLVEMENT--

I TRUST YOU TWO HAVE STOPPED BUTTIN' HEADS OVER THIS MISSION?

BASICALLY.

WE'RE FINE.

RIGHT THEN, LET'S *SUIT UP,* PEOPLE.

OUR TARGET IS IN POSSESSION OF THE COSMIC CUBE, SO SURPRISE IS *VITAL.* ALL WEAPONS SILENCED, ALL CONTACT OVER SECURE CHANNEL.

WE HIT THE GROUND RUNNING IN ONE MINUTE.

TANG!

THROK!

TEAM TWO, I WANT THOSE OUTER DOORS BLOWN-- NOW. MUTED DISRUPTER CHARGE.

UHHNN!

SMAK

I HAD THAT GUY.

I DON'T DOUBT IT...

I'M STILL MAD AT YOU. THIS DOESN'T CHANGE ANYTHING.

I DON'T DOUBT THAT, EITHER.

LET'S HEAR IT, KIRKMAN... GOOD NEWS *ONLY* THIS TIME.

THAT'S MOSTLY WHAT I'VE *GOT*, SIR. ALARM WAS NEUTRALIZED BEFORE IT SOUNDED, AND ALL SECURITY PERSONNEL ARE ACCOUNTED FOR.

NO CASUALTIES, BUT A FEW SERIOUS WOUNDED.

DOES LUKIN KNOW WE'RE COMIN' OR *NOT?*

ACCORDING TO THEIR SYSTEM, THEY'RE IN A SOUNDPROOF BOARDROOM ON THE 41ST FLOOR, AWAY FROM THE FRONT WINDOWS, BUT THEY PROBABLY FELT THAT *EXPLOSION.*

I'D GIVE OUR *ELEMENT OF SURPRISE* A CONSERVATIVE ESTIMATE OF ONE MORE MINUTE.

--UNDERSTAND ME? WHERE IS LUKIN'S *ASSASSIN?*

STEVE, LEAVE HIM, HE'S OUT OF IT.

CAP? YOU *COMIN'?* WE DON'T GOT A LOTTA TIME HERE.

YEAH...I'M COMING.

WE'LL FIND HIM, STEVE...*AFTER* WE GET LUKIN.

I KNOW.

I JUST WANT ANSWERS.

KIRKMAN?

LEFT END OF THE HALL. TWO GUARDS ON THE DOOR, *FACING* US.

NOT A PROBLEM.

SMAK

WAP

YOU'RE FROM THE *WHITE HOUSE?*

THAT'S RIGHT...THE KRONAS CORP RECENTLY BOUGHT OUT *ROXXON.* WE'RE HERE WORKING ON A DEAL FOR A PIPELINE FROM MADRIPOOR.

THIS MAN IS A *MASS-MURDERER!*

HE'S *RESPONSIBLE* FOR THE ATTACK IN PHILADELPHIA LAST WEEK!

THIS IS *OUTRAGEOUS!* HE *CAN'T* BE *SERIOUS?*

WHAT *IS* THIS, FURY? I THOUGHT THE PHILLY BOMBING WAS POINTING TO SOME ROGUE... JACK MARLOW OR SOMEBODY.

MONROE, SIR...AND WE BELIEVE HE WAS JUST A *SCAPEGOAT.*

DO YOU HAVE SOME *EVIDENCE* OF MR. LUKIN'S INVOLVEMENT, THEN?

NOT AT THIS TIME.

SO LET ME JUST GET THIS *STRAIGHT.*

YOU MOUNTED AN ASSAULT ON SOVEREIGN TERRITORY AGAINST AN IMPORTANT *FRIEND* TO THE U.S. *AND* THE U.N...ON A *HUNCH?*

YES SIR.

BUT THERE'S MORE *TO* IT THAN THAT...

I SHOULD HOPE THERE IS, COLONEL FURY...AND THE *SECRETARY-GENERAL* WILL WANT TO KNOW EXACTLY *WHAT* THAT IS WHEN YOU MEET WITH HIM *TOMORROW.*

OF COURSE, SIR.

ALL RIGHT, PEOPLE, *CLEAR OUT.*

NO!

WE ARE *NOT* LEAVING WITHOUT *LUKIN*, NICK!

YEAH, WE ARE.

ACTUALLY, CAPTAIN... YOU'RE LEAVING AFTER YOU *APOLOGIZE* TO MR. LUKIN.

WHAT?

STEVE, C'MON... LET IT *GO*. WE *LOST* THIS ONE.

I'M STILL *WAITING*, CAPTAIN...

THEN YOU CAN WAIT TILL *HELL* FREEZES OVER...AND TELL YOUR *BOSS* I'M DISAPPOINTED IN HIM.

THE UNITED STATES, OF COURSE, *FORMALLY* APOLOGIZES FOR THIS *INCIDENT*, ALEKSANDER... I CAN'T *IMAGINE* WHAT GOT INTO THEM.

BUT I *ASSURE YOU* THERE WILL BE *CONSEQUENCES*.

YES, I SHOULD *HOPE* SO...

AND WHAT EXACTLY WAS THE POINT OF *THAT*, ALEK?

YOU COULD HAVE COST US *EVERYTHING*...

YOU ARE BECOMING MORE LIKE A *WOMAN* EVERY DAY, LEON...SHOULD I MAKE THAT MORE THAN JUST A SIMILARITY OF *TEMPERAMENT*?

YOU? YOU *WOULDN'T*... HOW COULD YOU EVEN THREATEN--

RELAX, OLD FRIEND... I'M SORRY. YOU'RE *RIGHT*.

I DON'T KNOW WHAT CAME OVER ME.

THAT THING IS *CURSED*, ALEK... EVERY TIME YOU TOUCH IT I FEAR FOR YOUR SANITY.

DON'T BE *MELODRAMATIC*. I HAVE IT UNDER CONTROL, AND DON'T *WORRY* SO...

...I HAVE NO PLANS TO USE THE CUBE FOR OTHER THAN A FEW *SMALL THINGS*.

PROJECT WINTER SOLDIER: CONFIDENTIAL FILES

HEY...THIS IS JUST A SETBACK, STEVE...

IT WAS A *DISASTER.* LUKIN PLAYED US, *AGAIN*...LAUGHED IN OUR FACES.

YEAH, WELL...HE'S NOT *GOING* ANYWHERE.

HE DOESN'T *HAVE TO.* HE'S GOT THE CUBE... AND HE MAY AS WELL HAVE *DIPLOMATIC IMMUNITY.*

NO...I'M GONNA *NAIL* HIM. ONE WAY OR ANOTHER...

I HOPE SO, NICK... JUST SO I CAN SEE THAT GRIN WIPED OFF HIS *SMUG FACE.*

YOU'RE TOO *SOFT,* ROGERS...

...I WON'T BE HAPPY UNTIL I SEE THAT MAN *DEAD.*

UK!

YOU... KILLED HIM...

NICE'A YOU TO NOTICE.

OH GOD...ARE YOU GOING TO KILL ME?

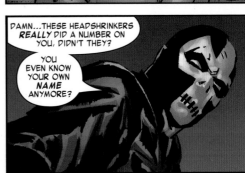

DAMN...THESE HEADSHRINKERS REALLY DID A NUMBER ON YOU, DIDN'T THEY?

YOU EVEN KNOW YOUR OWN NAME ANYMORE?

OF COURSE I DO...IT'S ERICA. ERICA HOLSTEIN.

NO, IT AIN'T. YOU'RE SYNTHIA SCHMIDT, GIRL...

...THE DAUGHTER OF THE RED SKULL.

DAMN IT TO HELL! WHERE HAS IT GOTTEN TO...?

PERHAPS YOU MISPLACED IT, ALEKSANDER?

DON'T BE AN IDIOT. THIS IS IMPORTANT.

WELL, IT DIDN'T JUST DISAPPEAR, DID IT?

WHAT HAVE YOU DONE? WHERE IS IT?

I HAVEN'T DONE ANYTHING... YOU'RE THE ONLY ONE WHO TOUCHED THAT FILE.

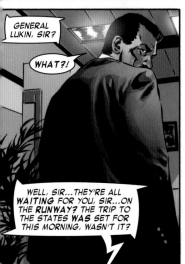

GENERAL LUKIN, SIR?

WHAT?!

WELL, SIR...THEY'RE ALL WAITING FOR YOU, SIR...ON THE RUNWAY? THE TRIP TO THE STATES WAS SET FOR THIS MORNING, WASN'T IT?

YES! YES! I KNOW ALL ABOUT IT, VALERI... THEY'RE JUST GOING TO HAVE TO WAIT UNTIL I'M READY!

YES, SIR... SORRY TO BOTHER YOU, SIR.

...WHAT HAVE YOU DONE...TO ME...?

Brooklyn, New York... Steve Rogers' Secret Residence

WHAT--?

SECURITY REPORT, LAST HOUR.

ALL ENTRIES SECURE. NO ACTIVITY.

NO SECURITY BREACH?

NEGATIVE. NO ACTIVITY.

SO, WHERE THE HELL DID *THIS* COME FROM, THEN...?

DAMN IT.

PROJECT WINTER SOLDIER: CONFIDENTIAL FILES

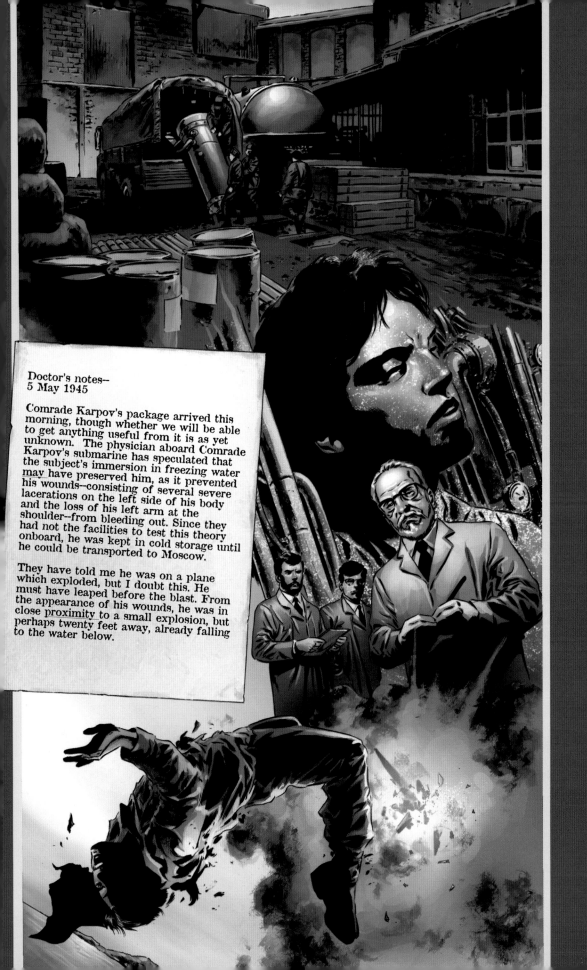

Doctor's notes--
5 May 1945

Comrade Karpov's package arrived this morning, though whether we will be able to get anything useful from it is as yet unknown. The physician aboard Comrade Karpov's submarine has speculated that the subject's immersion in freezing water may have preserved him, as it prevented his wounds--consisting of several severe lacerations on the left side of his body and the loss of his left arm at the shoulder--from bleeding out. Since they had not the facilities to test this theory onboard, he was kept in cold storage until he could be transported to Moscow.

They have told me he was on a plane which exploded, but I doubt this. He must have leaped before the blast. From the appearance of his wounds, he was in close proximity to a small explosion, but perhaps twenty feet away, already falling to the water below.

Tomorrow we will begin the process of allowing the subject's body to regain its heat, in the hope that his blood will still be viable for testing. We are using an approach for this that one of our spies smuggled out of Hitler's most secret laboratories.

I have not personally witnessed it, but have read of cases where a body that is flash-frozen has been completely revived. The case of the mother and child in Stalingrad frozen in a snowbank along the road for two hours, for example.

I have little hope that will be the case here, but Comrade Karpov and his superiors are more interested in the analysis of his vital fluids than in his revivification.

Apparently Comrade Karpov once saw the subject in action, and believes it probable that he, like his partner Captain America, has the much-rumored Super-Soldier Formula flowing through-- or rather, frozen inside-- his veins.

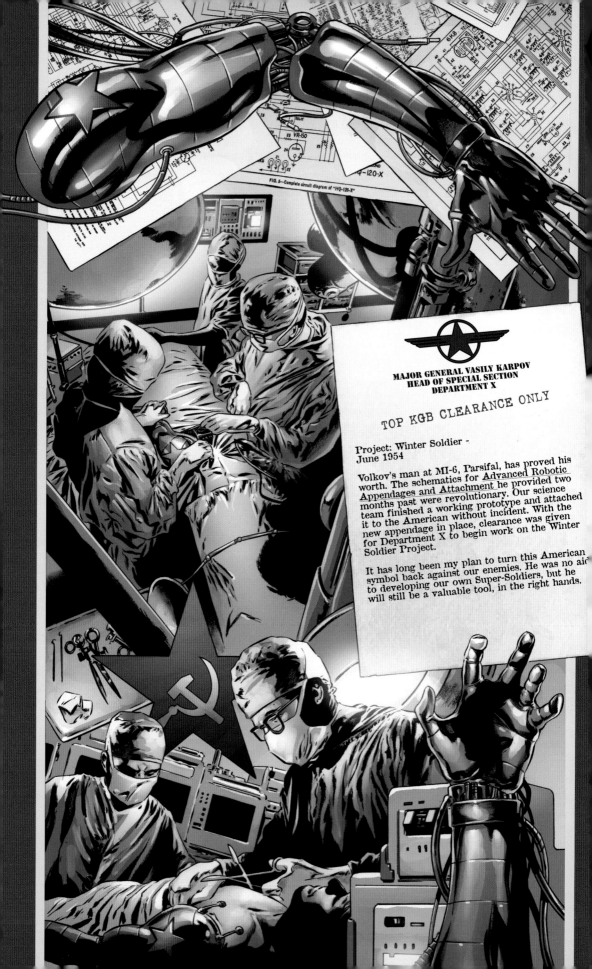

**MAJOR GENERAL VASILY KARPOV
HEAD OF SPECIAL SECTION
DEPARTMENT X**

TOP KGB CLEARANCE ONLY

Project: Winter Soldier -
June 1954

Volkov's man at MI-6, Parsifal, has proved his
worth. The schematics for Advanced Robotic
Appendages and Attachment he provided two
months past were revolutionary. Our science
team finished a working prototype and attached
it to the American without incident. With the
new appendage in place, clearance was given
for Department X to begin work on the Winter
Soldier Project.

It has long been my plan to turn this American
symbol back against our enemies. He was no aid
to developing our own Super-Soldiers, but he
will still be a valuable tool, in the right hands.

It was our own experiments in Mental Implantation during Sensory Deprivation that provided the breakthrough. And because of the American's memory loss, it was quite simple. We were able to reprogram the American's mind.

We gave him a purpose, and we made him loyal to no one but us.

Once that was accomplished, we had simply to train and prepare him for a field evaluation.

Hopes are high that he will be a successful operative. I believe, because he walks and talks just like them, because he exudes "America" with his every breath, that the enemy will never see him coming.

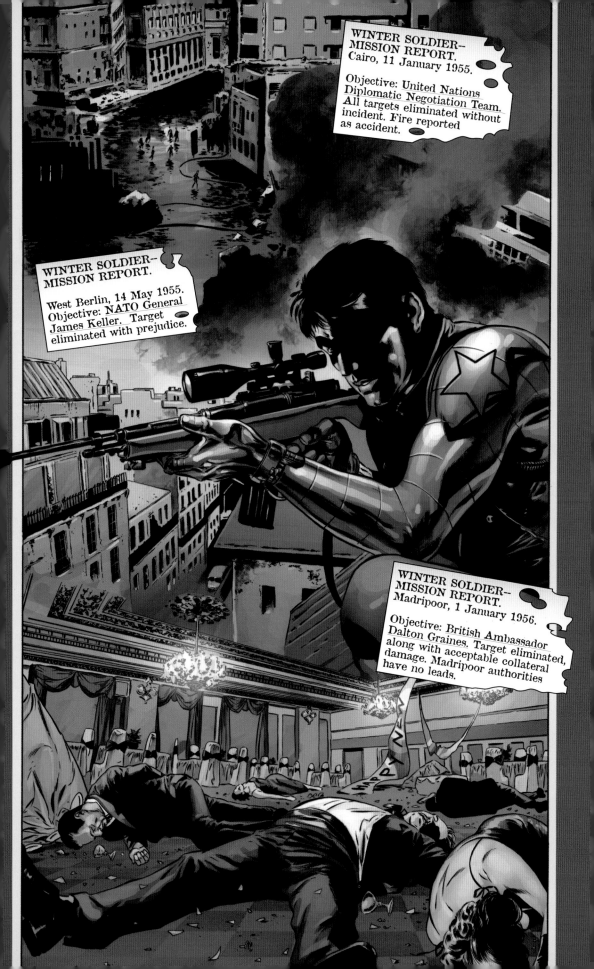

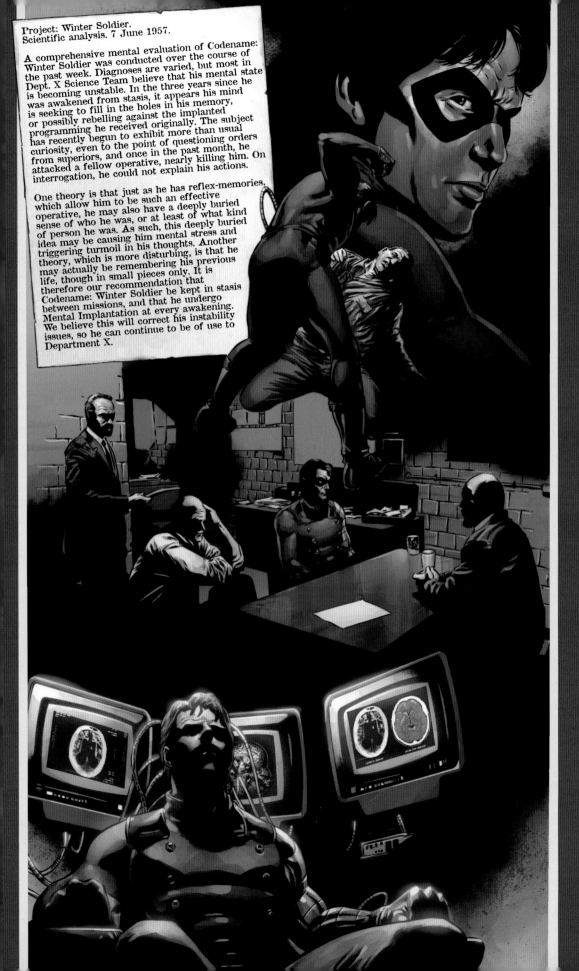

Project: Winter Soldier.
Scientific analysis. 7 June 1957.

A comprehensive mental evaluation of Codename:
Winter Soldier was conducted over the course of
the past week. Diagnoses are varied, but most in
Dept. X Science Team believe that his mental state
is becoming unstable. In the three years since he
was awakened from stasis, it appears his mind
is seeking to fill in the holes in his memory,
or possibly rebelling against the implanted
programming he received originally. The subject
has recently begun to exhibit more than usual
curiosity, even to the point of questioning orders
from superiors, and once in the past month, he
attacked a fellow operative, nearly killing him. On
interrogation, he could not explain his actions.

One theory is that just as he has reflex-memories,
which allow him to be such an effective
operative, he may also have a deeply buried
sense of who he was, or at least of what kind
of person he was. As such, this deeply buried
idea may be causing him mental stress and
triggering turmoil in his thoughts. Another
theory, which is more disturbing, is that he
may actually be remembering his previous
life, though in small pieces only. It is
therefore our recommendation that
Codename: Winter Soldier be kept in stasis
between missions, and that he undergo
Mental Implantation at every awakening.
We believe this will correct his instability
issues, so he can continue to be of use to
Department X.

Incident Report.
12 March 1973 re:
Codename: Winter Soldier

I regret to report that after more than fifteen years of selective use around the world, all to great success, last month's Winter Soldier mission into the United States did not go as planned.

The target, Senator Harry Baxtor, was eliminated, and the death was made to appear accidental. But after that, something went wrong.

Codename: Winter Soldier failed to appear at his extraction point.

His handlers waited, and listened in to police transmissions, but he did not arrive, and the local authorities reported nothing that implied he'd been apprehended.

From the Personal Journal of Major General Vasily Karpov-- September 1983

Against advice, I have taken Codename: Winter Soldier to the Middle East as my personal bodyguard. I am getting old and I know there are only a few years left for me, so I wish to spend them watching this twisted creature defend my life.

I almost feel sorry for him, as he tenses up whenever anyone approaches, ready to dive in front of a bullet for me.

It will never make up for what he and his people did to me in the war, how they shamed me in front of my own men, but even after all these years, it still makes me smile to see Captain America's partner serving Mother Russia.

Let us see what kind of damage he can do to his country's efforts in the Middle East. These next few years should be amusing. I am glad that Yuri transferred me. To hell with him.

FURY, I NEED YOU AND SHARON DOWN HERE *RIGHT NOW.*

I'VE GOT SOMETHING YOU NEED TO SEE... ABOUT THE WINTER SOLDIER.

WHAT IS IT, ROGERS?

YOU JUST HAVE TO SEE IT, NICK...TRUST ME.

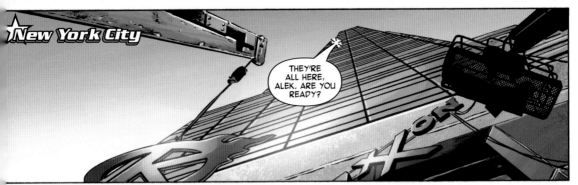

THEY'RE ALL HERE, ALEK. ARE YOU READY?

OF COURSE, LEON... AND GET THAT *WORRIED TONE* OUT OF YOUR VOICE.

I'M SORRY, BUT WE HAVE THE CEOs OF THE WORLD'S MOST POWERFUL COMPANIES WAITING... AND YOUR BEHAVIOR HAS BEEN *ERRATIC* LATELY.

IT'S THAT *THING*, I'M CERTAIN OF IT... WE SHOULD KEEP IT IN A CONTAINER. IT ISN'T SAFE...

LEON, YOU ARE MY OLDEST FRIEND, BUT IF YOU SPEAK LIKE THIS IN THE MEETING, I *WILL* KILL YOU. THAT'S A PROMISE.

GENTLEMEN... WELCOME TO THE *AMERICAN* OFFICES OF THE KRONAS CORPORATION.

IF WE HAVEN'T MET PREVIOUSLY, I AM ALEKSANDER LUKIN...

...AND *THIS* IS THE OBJECT YOU HAVE COME TO SEE.

SHALL WE OPEN BIDDING AT *ONE HUNDRED BILLION DOLLARS*?

AND YOU'VE GOT NO IDEA WHERE THIS CAME FROM?

NO, I'VE GOT A PRETTY DECENT *IDEA.*

BUY WAR BONDS

THE *CUBE?*

WHAT ELSE?

BUT *WHY?*

WHY HAS LUKIN DONE *ANY* OF THE THINGS HE'S DONE?

BONDS

TO MESS WITH YOUR *HEAD,* MOST LIKELY.

BUT THIS, IF HE REALLY *DID* PUT THIS HERE...IT'S LIKE HE'S TIPPING HIS HAND...

I KNOW.

STILL, IT *DOES* CONTINUE THE "MESSING WITH YOUR HEAD" THEME HE'S BEEN WORKIN'.

YEAH...IT DOES.

BUY WAR BONDS

WELL, LET'S SEE WHAT MY TECHS'VE GOT TO SAY ABOUT ITS AUTHENTICITY...

I'M ASSUMING YOU DON'T MIND IF I *TAKE IT?*

IT CAN'T GET OUT OF MY HOME *FAST ENOUGH,* NICK.

YEAH, THIS IS...*REALLY* MESSED UP.

IT'S A *NIGHTMARE.*

AND IT MATCHES UP WITH EVERYTHING ELSE WE *KNOW* ABOUT THE WINTER SOLDIER...

WHICH IS THE ONLY THING THAT'S STOPPING ME FROM TEARING IT TO PIECES.

BECAUSE YOU THINK IT'S THE *REAL* THING?

I DON'T WANT TO... BUT...

YOU REALIZE WHAT THIS *MEANS,* IF IT'S LEGIT?

WHAT?

THAT IT'S NOT *REALLY* BUCKY... IT'S JUST WHATEVER WAS LEFT OF HIM THAT THEY COULD *MANIPULATE* FOR THEIR OWN ENDS.

IS THAT SUPPOSED TO MAKE ME FEEL BETTER?

YEAH.

WELL, IT *DOESN'T*... AND YOU SHOULD READ THAT FILE *CLOSER*, SHARON.

HE KEPT TURNING *AGAINST* THEM, AND HE *DISAPPEARED* WHEN THEY SENT HIM TO AMERICA.

THERE'S SOME PART OF HIM, OF WHO HE IS, STILL *TRAPPED* INSIDE... SOMEWHERE INSIDE THAT *THING* THEY TURNED HIM INTO, IS WHATEVER'S *LEFT* OF BUCKY BARNES' *HUMANITY*.

WE DON'T KNOW THAT, ROGERS...

HE WAS MY *PARTNER*, DAMN IT...

...HE WAS MY *FRIEND*...

WHAT DO YOU THINK OF HIM?

WHICH ONE, THE KID?

YEAH, THE KID... WHO'S FOUR WHOLE YEARS YOUNGER THAN YOU, ROGERS.

NICE MOVES. I RECOGNIZE A FEW OF THEM.

YOU SHOULD. HE'S BEEN WORKING WITH THE SAME MEN WHO TRAINED YOU.

AND HE JUST GOT BACK FROM A MONTH IN THE U.K. WITH THAT S.A.S. REGIMENT THEY STARTED UP LAST YEAR...

SIR, YOU CAN'T BE THINKING... I MEAN... HE'S WHAT, SIXTEEN?

WE BOTH KNOW HE'S NOT THE ONLY SIXTEEN-YEAR-OLD IN THE ARMY, ROGERS.

AND HE'S ABOUT THE BEST NATURAL FIGHTER I'VE *EVER* SEEN. EVEN *BEFORE* HIS SPECIAL TRAINING.

WHAT'S HIS NAME?

JAMES BUCHANAN BARNES, GOES BY *BUCKY*. HIS OLD MAN WAS CAREER MILITARY, DIED A FEW YEARS AGO...

BUCKY'S BEEN LIVING HERE SINCE, SORT OF THE CAMP'S KID BROTHER.

WHEN WE TALKED ABOUT THIS BEFORE, ME NEEDING A PARTNER...I NEVER THOUGHT...

I KNOW. BUT JUST LIKE *CAPTAIN AMERICA* HAS SYMBOLIC VALUE, AN AMERICAN TEENAGER FIGHTING ALONGSIDE HIM... *THAT'S* A POWERFUL SYMBOL, TOO...

AND IF HE GETS HIS HANDS A LITTLE DIRTIER THAN *MOST* SOLDIERS WHEN NO ONE'S *LOOKING*... WELL, THAT'LL BE OUR *SECRET*, RIGHT?

ALL RIGHT, LET ME MEET HIM, AT LEAST...

STEVE...?

I THOUGHT YOU LEFT WITH FURY.

NO, I WAS HOPING YOU AND I COULD TALK...

I'M NOT REALLY IN A TALKING MOOD.

HOW ABOUT A LISTENING ONE, THEN?

NO, BECAUSE I KNOW WHAT YOU'RE GOING TO SAY.

OH, AND WHAT'S THAT?

YOU THINK BECAUSE HE'S GOT NO MEMORIES OF WHO HE USED TO BE... THAT HE'S JUST SOME PROGRAMMED ASSASSIN...

YOU THINK THAT MAKES IT OKAY TO KILL HIM.

IT'S **NOT** BUCKY...NOT IN ANY WAY THAT MATTERS.

NOT TO **YOU.**

ALL HE IS ARE THE PARTS THAT REMEMBER HOW TO **KILL**, STEVE. AND THAT'S WHAT HE'S **DOING**...I DON'T GIVE A DAMN ABOUT THE **SKULL**...

...BUT JACK MONROE, ALL THOSE PEOPLE IN PHILADELPHIA... NEAL--NEAL TAPPER...

THAT'S ALL **LUKIN'S** DOING, SHARON...YOU'RE BLAMING THE **GUN** INSTEAD OF THE PERSON PULLING THE **TRIGGER.**

I KNOW WHO'S **RESPONSIBLE.** BUT WHAT I'M TRYING TO TELL YOU IS, HE **ISN'T** YOUR PARTNER-- YOUR FRIEND-- ANYMORE.

AND IF YOU GO INTO THIS THINKING OF HIM LIKE THAT--

DON'T WORRY ABOUT ME.

HE **ALREADY** DIED, STEVE.

YEAH... I WAS **THERE.**

THAT DOESN'T CHANGE THE FACT THAT HE'S WALKING AROUND OUT THERE *RIGHT NOW*, UNDER THE CONTROL OF THE *EXACT* KIND OF PEOPLE HE SPENT HIS LIFE FIGHTING.

THAT'S NOT WHAT I'M SAYING...

I *KNOW* YOU'RE GOING THROUGH *HELL*, STEVE...I JUST WANT TO MAKE SURE WE ALL KNOW WHAT--

I DON'T KNOW *ANYTHING* ANYMORE, SHARON.

AND I'M BEGINNING TO WONDER IF I EVER *DID*.

NICK, YEAH... NO, I *BLEW* IT. I THINK I USED TO KNOW HOW TO *TALK* TO HIM, BUT...

YEAH. YEAH...MAKE THE CALL, IF YOU CAN...

"...MAYBE HE'LL HAVE BETTER LUCK THAN I DID..."

ONE HUNDRED AND TWENTY BILLION!

MATCHED! AND A THIRTY PERCENT SHARE IN STOCK OPTIONS!

ONE HUNDRED FIFTY!

WAIT! WAIT A DAMN SECOND!

JUST *HOLD ON*, LUKIN...YOU'RE *ENJOYING* THIS, SEEING US FALL ALL OVER OURSELVES...

BUT HOW DO WE EVEN KNOW THAT REALLY *IS* THE COSMIC CUBE?

YOU'RE PHILIP HOCKNEY, RIGHT? FROM CHEMAXONE?

YOU WERE THE *DECIDING VOTE* THAT REFUSED KRONAS' *BUY OUT* OFFER?

THAT'S *CORRECT*.

AND NOW YOU'D LIKE SOME KIND OF DEMONSTRATION THAT THIS REALLY IS WHAT I SAY IT IS?

I THINK WE'RE ALL OWED AT LEAST THAT, DON'T YOU?

WELL, YOU'D THINK THE FACT THAT YOU ARE ALL *HERE*, AT A SECRET MEETING TOGETHER, WOULD BE PROOF ENOUGH...

SINCE THERE'S *NEVER* BEEN A TIME WHEN YOU TRAVELED WITHOUT YOUR *SECURITY*...

AND I CAN ASSURE YOU IT WAS THE CUBE THAT MADE THAT SEEM LIKE A *WISE* IDEA...WHICH IT *WASN'T*.

BUT STILL, PERHAPS A MORE *CONCRETE* DEMONSTRATION *IS* IN ORDER...

ALEK!

UK...

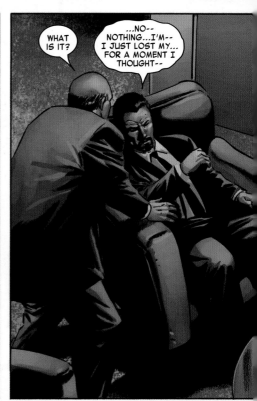

WHAT IS IT?

...NO-- NOTHING...I'M-- I JUST LOST MY... FOR A MOMENT I THOUGHT--

--I LOST MY...

THIS DAMNED THING!

YOU HONESTLY BELIEVE THIS MUCH POWER COMES WITH NO PRICE?

DON'T YOU TOUCH THAT!

ALEK?

DON'T YOU --!

KNNCH

DAMN IT.

THIS IS NO WAY TO FUNCTION... WORK THROUGH IT, STEVE.

ANGER WILL NOT HELP YOU DEAL WITH THIS.

IT'LL JUST MAKE SURE THAT *WHATEVER* YOU DO NEXT IS THE WRONG MOVE.

AND YOU CAN'T AFFORD THAT.

YOU'VE LET LUKIN PUSH ALL YOUR BUTTONS TOO EASILY SO FAR... YOU CAN'T AFFORD ANYTHING BUT A CLEAR HEAD FROM THIS POINT ON...

HE'S COUNTING ON YOU...WHETHER HE *KNOWS IT* OR NOT.

BUCKY IS COUNTING ON YOU.

Arnhem, The Netherlands
September 1944

IT'S *NO GOOD*, CAP! WE CAN'T *HOLD IT!*

BUDDA BUDDA BUDDA

OUR INTEL SAYS THE RED SKULL IS ENCAMPED *SOMEWHERE* ALONG THE RHINE, SO...

...WE'RE GONNA HELP THE BRITISH TAKE THAT *BRIDGE*, BUCK... ONE WAY OR ANOTHER.

LOOK AT THEM, THEY'VE LOST TOO MANY MEN, CAP...

THEY AREN'T GONNA BE ABLE TO DO THIS...

I KNOW... DAMN IT...

HEY... WHAT IN THE HELL?

NOOOO!

HEY-- HEY! STOP IT! NO!

AND SO IS *EVERYBODY ELSE...COUNTING ON ME.*

TH-WANNG

LIKE THE AMERICAN PEOPLE...

...WHO HE *KILLED* HUNDREDS OF, NOT A MONTH AGO.

WHAT...?

NO, IT WASN'T HIM. THAT WAS NOT HIS FAULT. NONE OF IT IS.

DON'T FORGET THAT.

FAP!

HE'S NOT RESPONSIBLE FOR HIS ACTIONS...NOT IN CONTROL.

HE'S NOT IN CONTROL...

...AND HE'D HATE THAT MORE THAN ANYTHING.

AW, CAP... THOSE SICK NAZI SONS OF--

I KNOW.

...CLIVE... M'MATE...

WHAT'S HE SAYING?

...WOT 'APPENED T' CLIVE...? WUZ ME BEST... BEST...

WE'VE GOT TO *MOVE*, BUCKY... NOW.

DAMN IT. THIS IS JUST-- FREAKIN' KRAUTS CUT UP THEIR *BRAINS*, STEVE...

THIS IS...IT'S-- IT'S *SICK*.

THAT'S REALLY THE PROBLEM, ISN'T IT? I KNOW WHAT BUCKY WOULD DO IN THIS SITUATION.

I KNOW WHAT HE'D *WANT*...

HE'D WANT ME TO DO WHATEVER IT TOOK TO STOP HIM.

GOD, I CAN'T BELIEVE I'M EVEN *THINKING* THAT SHARON MIGHT BE RIGHT.

THAT I MIGHT HAVE TO--

NO.

THERE HAS TO BE ANOTHER WAY OUT...HE'S STILL--

HEY, YOU'RE NOT GONNA *JUMP OFF* HERE, ARE YA?

'CAUSE IT TOOK ME HALF THE NIGHT TO FIND YOU...

...AN' I PRACTICALLY HAD TO TALK TO EVERY PIGEON IN NEW YORK STATE TO DO IT, MAN.

FALCON?

YEP...GOT A CALL FROM NICK FURY, SAID YOU MIGHT NEED A *FRIEND.*

YEAH... YEAH, I REALLY DO, SAM.

--SO HE *SHOULD* BE STABLE FOR NOW, SIR.

WHAT ABOUT *BRAIN DAMAGE?* CAN YOU TELL?

IT'S A LITTLE *EARLY* STILL. WE NEED TO SEE HOW MUCH OF THAT *SWELLING* GOES AWAY FIRST.

I'M MORE WORRIED ABOUT SAVING THAT *EYE*, FRANKLY.

I *SEE...*

DAMN IT. THIS *CANNOT* CONTINUE...

AND HERE I THOUGHT *MY LIFE* WAS *COMPLICATED.*

I MEAN, FURY GAVE A *FEW* DETAILS, BUT, *DAMN*...THAT'S A *SERIOUS* MIND-%#$ YOU'RE TALKIN' ABOUT, STEVE.

OH, BELIEVE ME, I *KNOW.*

AND YOU THINK THIS LUKIN GUY IS OUT FOR *REVENGE* ON YOU FROM BACK WHEN HE WAS A *KID?*

YET HE WAITS OVER TEN YEARS *AFTER* YOU COME OUT OF THE ICE TO MAKE A MOVE?

GOTTA BE SOMETHIN' *ELSE* GOIN' ON THERE...

UNLESS HE NEEDED THE *CUBE* FOR HIS PLAN TO WORK, SOMEHOW.

YEAH, THE COSMIC CUBE...REALLY HOPED I'D NEVER HAVE TO HEAR *THOSE WORDS* AGAIN.

YOU AND I ONLY MET *BECAUSE* OF THAT CUBE, SAM.

AND ONE OF THE *MANY TIMES* THE SKULL'S PLANS FOR IT WENT *WRONG.*

YOU EVER *NOTICE* HOW THAT WORKS? NO ONE'S *EVER* BEEN ABLE TO USE THAT DAMN THING AND HAVE IT TURN OUT THE WAY THEY *WANT.*

LIKE ALL THOSE BAD JOKES ABOUT THE GUY WHO FINDS THE *MAGIC LANTERN.*

IT DOES SEEM LIKE THAT... BUT WE CAN'T ASSUME IT'LL BE THAT WAY FOR *LUKIN.*

CONSIDERING HOW *FLAWLESSLY* HIS MOVES HAVE BEEN EXECUTED SO FAR...

HOW EASILY HE'S BEEN ABLE TO GET UNDER MY SKIN.

HE'S GOT *ADVANTAGES* THERE, STEVE...ONE IN *PARTICULAR.*

BUCKY...

YEP. GOT YOU THINKIN' YOU MIGHT HAVE TO PUT WHATEVER'S *LEFT* OF HIM OUT OF ITS *MISERY.* NO WAY THAT'S *NOT* GOING TO RIP YOU UP INSIDE...

...MAKE YOU QUESTION YOURSELF IN CIRCLES...

BUT THE ONLY QUESTION THAT REALLY *MATTERS,* STEVE, IS WHAT DO YOU WANT TO *DO?*

SAVE HIM... SOMEHOW.

GOOD. SO, HOW DO WE *DO* THAT?

--YOU'RE NOT TO LET ANYONE *ELSE* HANDLE THE *PACKAGE*, DO YOU UNDERSTAND ME?

YES, SIR.

THAT'S THE *MOST* IMPORTANT DETAIL. THIS ISN'T LIKE THE *LAST TIME* YOU CARRIED IT.

NOW IT'S GOT POWER--*REAL* POWER.

YOU'RE TO *KILL* ANY MAN WHO EVEN *ATTEMPTS* TO TOUCH IT.

WHATEVER YOU *SAY*, SIR.

WAS THAT A *TONE* THERE...IN YOUR *VOICE?*

I GUESS SO, SIR. JUST SEEMS LIKE A *WASTE* TO ME.

WE WENT TO A LOT OF TROUBLE TO GET IT, AND NOW YOU JUST WANT TO *BURY* THE THING.

EEPING SOMETHING
IS POWERFUL OUT
F THE HANDS OF MY
NEMIES IS A WAY OF
CONTROLLING IT.

ANY REASONS
BEYOND THAT
ARE MY CONCERN,
NOT YOURS.

OF
COURSE,
SIR.

THIS ISN'T
THE FIRST TIME
YOU'VE QUESTIONED
MY ORDERS,
SOLDIER.

SEE
THAT IT'S
THE LAST.

SIR,
YES SIR.

SENDING
THE CUBE AWAY,
ALEKSANDER?

THAT'S A
MISTAKE.

I'VE
DONE WHAT
I NEEDED
WITH IT...

IT'S A BIG
MISTAKE.

NO...
...THAT
THING IS
CURSED.

--TELLIN' YOU, FREIDMAN, GET *OUTTA* THERE.

YOU SO MUCH AS PUT A *SCRATCH* ON THAT PROTOTYPE AND YOU'RE GONNA HAVE THE *LEADERS* TO ANSWER TO.

OH, I'M *REEAAAALLY* SCARED NOW.

YOU SHOULD BE.

FACE IT, WE'RE A *JOKE* WITHOUT THE SKULL. WE EVEN HAVE A JOKE NAME...A.I.D.

SOUNDS *REAL* THREATENING...NOT.

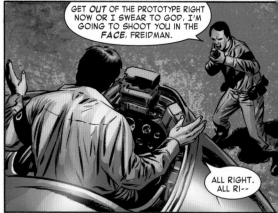

GET *OUT* OF THE PROTOTYPE RIGHT NOW OR I SWEAR TO GOD, I'M GOING TO SHOOT YOU IN THE *FACE*, FREIDMAN.

ALL RIGHT. ALL RI--

STATUS?

ALL CLEAR.

ANY *READINGS* ON WHAT'S BEHIND THOSE DOORS?

CROSS-REFERENCING BUILDING SCHEMATICS WITH SATELLITE READINGS AS WE SPEAK.

IT'S NOT CROWDED *YET*, BUT NEARLY EVERY WARM BODY IN THE BUILDING IS MOVING IN OUR DIRECTION, FAST.

GOOD. ISOLATE THE ONES THAT *AREN'T*.

OUR GUYS'LL BE THE ONES RUNNING FOR THE *EXITS*.

...HUH...?

HANG ON, STEVE...I'VE GOT THIS...

FALCON AND I'LL HANDLE *THIS*, IRON MAN.

YOU JUST CONCENTRATE ON FINDING OUR TARGETS.

I CAN DO BOTH, STEVE... EVER HEAR OF MULTI-TASKING?

LET'S NOT GET HUNG UP ON DETAILS...

...WE GOT *WORK* TO DO.

OHGODOHGODOHGOD!!

SHOOT TO KILL! KILL THEM!

SOMEONE GET THE PLASMA CANNON!

KUNNCH

CAP, I'VE GOT A **LOCK**. THREE MEN, HEADING FOR THE ROOF.

ROOF ACCESS LEADS TO A BUILDING AROUND THE BLOCK THAT APPEARS TO HAVE **SEVERAL** HELICOPTERS IN THE LOADING BAY.

GO.

I'M GONE.

FZZT

I KNEW THIS THING WOULD BE AWESOME...

NEXT!

BBZAATT

OOOFF!

UNH...

KRAKK

ZZUUNNG

DAMN IT! CAP! HEADS UP!

AID

YYYEEAAAAAAHHH!

BBZAATT

HEY--

AAAAAAAAA-

-AAAAAAHHHHH!

SHHRRAAAK

CLEARLY, THAT IS NOT A TOY, MORON.

OH GOD OH GOD OH GOD OH GOD...

NICE WORK...

...BUT CHECK THIS OUT... CAUGHT ME A CREEPY LITTLE MAD-SCIENTIST GUY.

WHAT-- WHAT DO YOU--

I--I'M NOT--NOT--

OH G-GOD... WHAT DO YOU WANT?

SIMPLE. I WANT YOU TO TELL ME HOW TO TRACK A COSMIC CUBE.

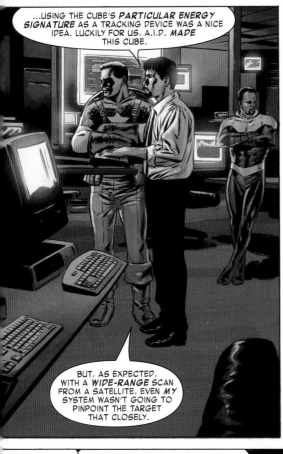

...USING THE CUBE'S *PARTICULAR ENERGY SIGNATURE* AS A TRACKING DEVICE WAS A NICE IDEA. LUCKILY FOR US, A.I.D. *MADE* THIS CUBE.

BUT, AS EXPECTED, WITH A *WIDE-RANGE* SCAN FROM A SATELLITE, EVEN *MY* SYSTEM WASN'T GOING TO PINPOINT THE TARGET THAT CLOSELY.

EXCEPT WE GOT LUCKY *AGAIN*, BECAUSE THE SIGNAL'S *MOVING* FAST. MUST BE IN A JET.

WHERE'S IT *GOING*?

THAT'S WHERE IT GETS COMPLICATED. TRAJECTORY APPEARS SOUTH-SOUTHWEST, SO...

...I OVERLAID ITS PROJECTED *FLIGHT PATH* WITH LOCATIONS OF KRONAS HOLDINGS, AND LOOK AT *THIS*...

A NEXTGEN *RESEARCH* FACILITY THAT KRONAS RECENTLY PURCHASED.

WHY WOULD THEY BE TAKING THE CUBE THERE?

I DON'T KNOW. IT'S AN UNDERGROUND FACILITY THAT NEXTGEN HASN'T USED FOR *YEARS*.

BUT IT *DOES* HAVE A NUCLEAR-SAFE *VAULT* EVEN FURTHER BELOW THE SURFACE, FOR KEEPING IN-DEVELOPMENT PROJECTS SAFE FROM CORPORATE THEFT.

SO, FOR SOME REASON, THE PSYCHOTIC EX-SOVIET GENERAL IS TAKING THE COSMIC CUBE TO A *FALLOUT SHELTER?*

THIS SOUND LIKE *TROUBLE* TO ANYONE BUT ME?

YEAH. WE'VE GOT TO *GO.*

UH...

WHAT?

I SAID, THIS IS WHERE IT GOT *COMPLICATED,* AND IT DOES, BECAUSE I *CAN'T* GO WITH YOU.

I BARELY *FOUGHT OFF* A TAKEOVER FROM KRONAS LAST MONTH.

HAD TO PERSONALLY CONVINCE HALF THE BOARD TO VOTE *AGAINST IT,* THE MONEY WAS SO GOOD.

AND AFTER THE HIT OUR *STOCK* TOOK WHEN THE AVENGERS IMPLODED, IF *IRON MAN* IS PART OF A *RAID* ON A KRONAS FACILITY--

YOU COULD *LOSE* YOUR COMPANY?

TO PUT IT BLUNTLY-- YES.

THE BOARD WOULD SEE IT AS CORPORATE WARFARE AND TURN ON ME.

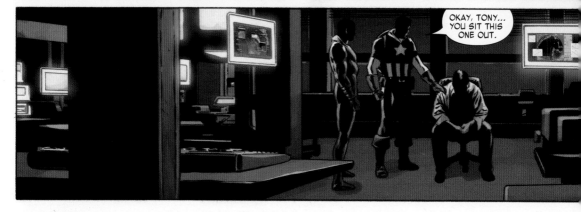

OKAY, TONY... YOU SIT THIS ONE OUT.

BAD MOVE, STEVE...*SERIOUSLY* BAD MOVE.

...YING HEAD-ON [A]T THE COSMIC [C]UBE, COULD'VE *REALLY* USED [I]RON MAN FOR *BACKUP.*

AND LET HIM LOSE EVERYTHING HE'S SPENT HIS LIFE BUILDING? NO... TONY'S DOING *IMPORTANT* WORK, FOR THE FUTURE.

WON'T *BE* MUCH FUTURE IF THIS LUKIN GUY GOES *BIBLICAL* WITH THE CUBE.

WE'LL TAKE CARE OF IT.

WE'RE *GOOD,* SURE... BUT WE'VE GOT NO IDEA WHAT WE'RE--

B-DEET-DEET! B-DEET-DEET!

HANG ON.

AM I *CRAZY,* OR DID YOU AND YOUR FRIENDS TAKE OUT AN A.I.D. WAREHOUSE THIS MORNING?

I WAS JUST ABOUT TO CALL YOU ABOUT THAT, SHARON.

HOW DID YOU EVEN *FIND* THEM?

WASN'T HARD. TONY STARK JUST USED A FEW OF HIS *SLEAZIER* BUSINESS CONNECTIONS.

AND I'M ASSUMING THERE WAS A *PURPOSE* TO THIS?

STANDS TO REASON WHEREVER THE CUBE IS, LUKIN WILL HAVE IT UNDER GUARD BY HIS *BEST* PEOPLE...

...AND THAT'LL *INCLUDE* THE WINTER SOLDIER.

SO, I NEEDED SOMEONE TO TELL ME HOW TO *FIND* THE CUBE.

THEY KNEW *HOW*? THEN WHY NOT JUST STEAL IT BACK?

BECAUSE THEY KNOW WHAT IT *IS*, TOO, SO THEY AREN'T IN ANY RUSH TO *ANGER* ITS OWNER.

SO WHAT *DID* YOU FIND OUT?

THAT LUKIN IS TAKING THE CUBE TO AN UNDERGROUND RESEARCH FACILITY IN THE MOUNTAINS OF WEST VIRGINIA.

I JUST SENT YOU EVERYTHING WE'VE GOT. SAM AND I ARE PRESENTLY EN ROUTE.

I DON'T KNOW WHAT THEY'RE UP TO, BUT WE'VE GOT TO STOP THEM BEFORE THEY ACCESS THE DEEP-STORAGE VAULT.

STARK

YOU'RE ALREADY--? YOU SHOULD'VE CALLED ME *SOONER*.

SO FURY CAN GET TIED UP IN *RED TAPE* AGAIN? NO THANKS.

JUST CONSIDER THIS A *RELIABLE TIP* THAT THERE'S A WEAPON OF MASS DESTRUCTION AT THE COORDINATES I JUST SENT YOU.

ROGERS OUT.

DAMN IT...

THIS IS AGENT 13. I NEED A *STRIKE TEAM* READY... NOW.

--CLOSE AS WE'RE GONNA GET WITHOUT BEING SEEN.

MAN, SHARON SOUNDED LIKE A REAL HARD#*$ THERE...

WHATEVER *HAPPENED* TO THE OLD HAPPY-GO-LUCKY SHARON?

HER LAST BOYFRIEND WAS *KILLED* IN THE PHILADELPHIA BOMBING.

OH.

AND SHE WAS NEVER *THAT* HAPPY-GO-LUCKY.

BUT SHE *DID* USED TO SMILE MORE OFTEN...

SO, WE GOT A *PLAN*, OR ARE WE JUST RUSHIN' IN BLIND?

WE'RE *NOT* RUSHING IN *BLIND*, THAT'S FOR SURE.

THIS ISN'T THE FIRST TIME YOU'VE *QUESTIONED* MY ORDERS, SOLDIER.

SEE THAT IT'S THE *LAST.*

"YOU'RE TO *KILL* ANY MAN WHO EVEN *ATTEMPTS* TO TOUCH IT.

"...KILL ANY MAN WHO..."

BLAM

NO WAY DID I MISS...

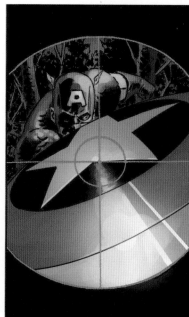

CAP--ABOVE THE *ENTRANCE,* THREE O'CLOCK!

BIRDS SPOTTED HIM!

BLAM

GOT IT!

MOVE IN, SAM-- *GO!*

SMAK

EX-SPETSNAZ? YOU GUYS AIN'T %#$!

GET HIM! TAKE HIM DOWN!

AW, DAMN...

RATATATATATAT

SECURE THAT ENTRANCE, AND I WANT THREE OF YOU RUNNING A SWEEP INSIDE--NOW!

YES, MA'AM.

YOU'RE *STILL* HERE? THAT PUNCH SHOULD'VE PUT YOU DOWN FOR *GOOD*.

SMAK

...TRIED TO *KILL* ME...

IS THIS *REALLY* ALL YOU *ARE* NOW?

IS THERE NO PART OF YOU THAT KNOWS WHAT YOU USED TO *BE*?

SHUT UP!

YOU WERE *BETTER* THAN THIS!

SHUT UP!

YOU DON'T *KNOW* ME!

KSSSHH

YOU WERE SUPPOSED TO BE *TOUGH*, BUT THIS IS...*WEAK!*

REMEMBER WHO I AM?!

THE ONLY THING I AM--

SECURE VAULT ACCESS

--IS THE MAN WHO'S GONNA *KILL YOU!*

FINE...

...THEN *GO* AHEAD.

SHOOT ME.

IF YOU TRULY DON'T KNOW ME...

...THEN JUST DO IT.

...NO... NO...

IT'S OKAY, BUCK...IT'S GOING TO BE OKAY...

STEVE... STEP *AWAY* FROM HIM!

SHARON... IT'S *OVER.* LET IT GO. THIS *ISN'T* THE MAN WHO KILLED YOUR FRIEND.

NOT ANYMORE.

CAP...?

WHAT-- WHAT'D YOU *DO...?*

HOW CAN I...? NO...YOU SHOULD'VE JUST...

...KILLED ME.

WHAT?

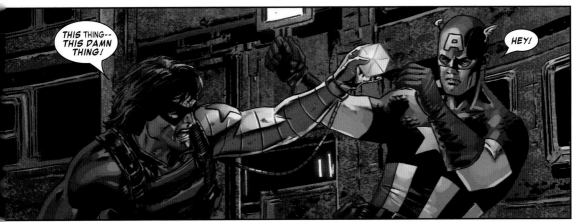

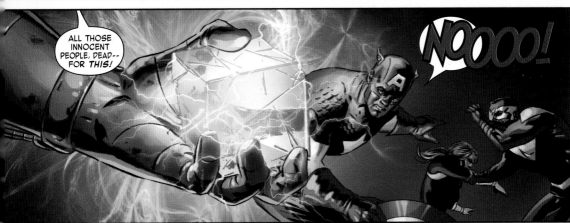

...NO...

DAMN IT... NO...

IS HE...?

YOU HEARD WHAT HE *SAID* RIGHT BEFORE HE GRABBED IT... WHATTA YOU THINK?

NO...HE'S *NOT* DEAD...HE JUST-- HE ISN'T.

I THINK SAM'S *RIGHT*, STEVE...HE COULDN'T LIVE WITH WHAT THEY'D *DONE* TO HIM...

HE *WANTED* TO DIE.

NO... BUCKY'S A SURVIVOR...

WELCOME TO FORT LEHIGH US ARMY

"...HE'S OUT THERE, SOMEWHERE... I KNOW IT."

PRIVATE BARNES... YOU STAND AT *ATTENTION* WHEN IN THE PRESENCE OF *OFFICERS!*

SIR, YES SIR!

THAT'S MORE LIKE IT... NOW I'VE BROUGHT SOMEONE I WANT YOU TO MEET...

THIS IS CORPORAL STEVE ROGERS, ALSO KNOWN AS *CAPTAIN AMERICA*...

...IF YOU CAN PASS *MUSTER*, YOU'RE GOING TO BE HIS PARTNER.

"YOU'RE A FOOL..."

...I TOLD YOU IT WAS A *MISTAKE* TO SEND THE CUBE AWAY, ALEKSANDER.

AND NOW YOU'VE *LOST* IT.

I'M NOT *CONCERNED*... IT'S JUST AS *WELL* IT'S BEEN DESTROYED, IF YOU ASK ME.

IT'S ONE OF THE MOST POWERFUL OBJECTS IN THE *UNIVERSE*, AND YOU SIMPLY THROW IT AWAY...BECAUSE YOU HURT YOUR *FRIEND?* SUCH A WEAKLING.

YOU COULD HAVE RESTORED HIM TO FULL HEALTH WITH JUST A *THOUGHT*...

AND BROUGHT BACK YOUR PRECIOUS SOCIALIST REPUBLIC WITH NOT MUCH MORE EFFORT.

NO. I'VE LEARNED SOMETHING *YOU* NEVER COULD...THAT *NOTHING* YOU WISH FOR WITH THAT THING GOES *WELL*.

THAT CUBE IS *CURSED*...LOOK WHAT IT'S DONE TO ME, AFTER ALL...

...PUTTING A CREATURE LIKE *YOU* INSIDE MY MIND.

AND IF IT'D HAD MORE POWER THAT NIGHT, I'D BE THE *ONLY ONE* HERE, ALEKSANDER...

YOU GOT *LUCKY.*

OR WE *BOTH* GOT CURSED...TRAPPED TOGETHER...

...LIKE RATS IN A CAGE.

YES... FOR *NOW*...

⭐ **The End**

THE ARTIST
Steve Epting

Steve Epting is a winner. Quite literally. Of a competition that never existed.

Graduating with a Bachelor of Fine Arts degree in graphic design from the University of South Carolina, Steve Epting soon found work. But not in comic books. He began working as a graphic designer in the late 80s, when he read in the local press that publisher **First Comics** were holding a competition at the nearby **Atlanta Fantasy Fair** for the best new comics creators and would publish the best six-page story as a back-up strip in one of their comics.

Only trouble is, First Comics didn't know anything about it. They did however promise to look at the work of the entrants to make up for the mistake, including that of Steve Epting, who they declared joint winner – even though there was no prize any more. But it did lead Epting to have a long chat at the show with First's art director. And as a result, Epting actually got work out of it. He began drawing comic books.

He originally worked on First books such as *Whisper, Dreadstar* and *Hammer Of The Gods* until First Comics folded. At which point Epting was able to use his now-considerable portfolio of work to get started at **Marvel.** A one-off issue of *The Avengers* led him to become the regular artist on the book in a run still highly thought-of today. During the mid 90s, he left the book to work on a number of *X-Men* mini-series and specials, before jumping across the street at the end of the decade to **DC** where he worked on *Aquaman*.

It was then that he made the move to upstart publisher **CrossGen,** trying to make itself a competitor for both Marvel and DC. Grabbing a lot of big names to work on their books, CrossGen demanded that creators move to Tampa in Florida and work out of the company's offices in a collaborative fashion. Epting worked here for over two years, drawing twenty-five issues of *Crux* written by **Mark Waid,** before co-creating his own book with **Chuck Dixon,** the pirate comic *El Cazador,* to rave reviews. Six issues in however, CrossGen closed, declaring bankruptcy.

So Epting returned to Marvel, and found himself working with **Ed Brubake**r on *Captain America*, on what would become a legendary run on the character, including the *Death Of Captain America* issue

that caused so much fuss in the media (and so many sales as well). Epting and Brubaker's run also influenced the development of the Cap movie and much of their take on the character can be seen on the screen as a result.

Currently, he is drawing *Fantastic Four* and *FF,* written by **Jonathan Hickman,** in which he also killed off the **Human Torch.** He's suddenly turned into the artist assassin of the Marvel Universe.

So the big question is... where will Steve Epting go next – and who will he kill off when he gets there? Spider-Man, start shaking in your boots!

THE WRITER
Ed Brubaker

Photo by Luigi Novi

LIFE EXPERIENCE

There's probably no such thing as a typical rise to become a superhero comic book writer. But even given that, Ed Brubaker's career seems rather atypical.

Born in 1966 in Maryland, he first encountered comics when his father brought some home from the naval base in which he worked, to encourage his reading. It seemed to have the right effect and in his late teens, Ed Brubaker started writing and drawing them too. His early breakout hit was a comic called *Lowlife*, published by small press **Slave Labor.** Fitting in to the nineties trend for slice-of-life and autobiographical comic books, Ed Brubaker wrote about himself and his life as a petty criminal. It was honest, raw, unflinching and brave.

So it wasn't too much of a jump when he started writing about other criminal lives for *Dark Horse Presents* including the serial *An Accidental Death,* drawn by Eric Shanower, that saw Ed nominated for an Eisner Award, the most prestigious English language comics prize.

As a result of the win, he was snapped up by **DC Comics,** who first used him on their mature readers **Vertigo** comics line, working on political satire *Prez.* It was nagging from Vertigo editor Shelly Bond for a new comic that saw him pitch something outside of Vertigo's usual mix of fantasy, horror and satire, a straightforward crime series called *Scene Of The Crime* published in 1999, with Michael Lark and Sean Phillips, two artists who Brubaker would work with extensively in the future. It was a critical hit and saw DC offer Brubaker an exclusive contract.

Which means he got to work with their superheroes. And while you can take the man out of crime, you can't take crime out of the man. Writing *Batman* and *Catwoman* he gave the books a harder, street edge. He would do the same for **DC's Wildstorm** imprint on *Point Blank,* starring Grifter.

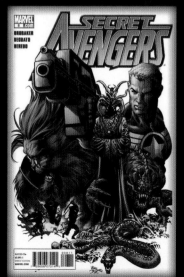

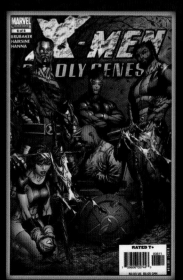

But it would be working with Greg Rucka and Michael Lark on *Gotham Central* that would take this to a new level, telling the story of the police who work in Gotham, dealing with supervillains and superheroes as part of their day job, and with Sean Phillips on *Sleeper*, the story of Grifter's brother and the criminal underworld.

CRIMINAL MASTERMIND

Brubaker was now your go-to guy for gritty, criminal storytelling. And **Marvel** came calling. No longer exclusive to DC, in 2005 Marvel hired Ed Brubaker to write *Captain America*, with Steve Epting on art. He was a hit, as the book gained massive newspaper coverage for the infamous **Death Of Captain America** story. Signing an exclusive with Marvel, he was allowed to finish his runs on *Gotham Central* and *Sleeper* for DC, and won his first Eisner Award as Best Writer. It would not be his last.

CAP CONNECTIONS

It's interesting to note that Brubaker's first association with Marvel's Sentinel of Liberty was actually in the late 70s when he had a letter printed in an issue of Captain America. He even won a much sought-after Marvel No-Prize!

He then expanded his role at Marvel, working on *Daredevil* with Michael Lark, a number of X-Men projects and was then given the ultimate reward at Marvel, his own creator-owned books. Created with Sean Phillips, *Criminal* and *Incognito* were raw, uncompromising crime books, the first looking at brothers pulled into crime, and the second a look at the witness protection programme from the point of view of a super villain.

But he has kept on writing *Captain America*, now working on two series, the new relaunched version with artist Steve McNiven that coincided with the movie's release, and *Captain America And Bucky* with Chris Samnee, set during World War II and following the life of Bucky as he becomes Captain America's sidekick. And more awards, acclaim and sales have followed.

Right now there doesn't seem to be any reason for him to stop writing America's leading patriot. Indeed, it would be a crime.

ORIGINS...
Bucky

BOY SOLDIER

When *Captain America Comics* was first published at the end of 1940, America had not entered World War II. Nevertheless, Cap was seen on the cover, punching out Adolf Hitler and leading an assault against the Nazi threat. But he wasn't alone. Right from the beginning, Bucky was at his side, created by **Joe Simon** and **Jack Kirby** and published by **Timely Comics** which, twenty years later, would be known as **Marvel.** Full name James Buchanan Barnes, his nickname Bucky was taken from Joe Simon's childhood friend Bucky Pierson.

He didn't have the powers of Captain America. But Bucky fulfilled the classic role of the kid sidekick – brave, fearless with a light, chirpy attitude. The idea of the kid sidekick was that such a character would be relatable to the target audience, as a way to get into the stories of the older, lead superhero. The sidekick also allowed for easy exposition, Captain America was able to explain the Nazi-fighting narrative to Bucky - and the readers - as it unfolded, without having to talk to himself, or use acres of thought balloons.

And so the duo fought Nazis in Europe and then, after the assault on Pearl Harbour, took on the Japanese. However, Bucky was injured in 1948, shot down in battle, and replaced by a female counterpart and girlfriend for Captain America, **Betsy Ross,** otherwise known as **Golden Girl.** The time for kid sidekicks was over, for a while at least, as the post war glamour of the romantic movies spilled over into comic books and romance was the big thing. Bucky would briefly return in the 1950s Captain America comic, where the two would fight communist threats.

MAN OUT OF TIME

But it was the now-named Marvel Comics that would bring back Captain America in *The Avengers* comic in the 1960s. **Stan Lee** and Captain America's original co-creator **Jack Kirby** rewrote history so that Cap went missing at the end of World War II, Bucky died, and the commie-smashing 50s Bucky and Cap were different characters entirely posing as the famous pair.

CAP AND BUCKY IN THE FIFTIES

Bucky's fifties doppleganger was explained as **Jack Monroe**, an orphan who discovered his history teacher had a passion for Captain America - to the extent that he reshaped his face to look like him and changed his name to Steve Rogers. They both discovered the super serum that gave Captain America his powers and used it to take down communists – or whoever they believed to be communists, as the serum affected their minds. Taken down by the FBI, Monroe would later recover, and take another of Steve Rogers's superhero identities, that of Nomad.

Captain America went on to lead the Avengers. And Bucky went on to... still be dead. Over the next fifty years, Bucky was famously one of the only characters in the Marvel Universe who would not return from the great beyond. We would see Bucky in time travel stories, flashbacks, tales from the past and as an occasional zombie. Various other characters would take the role of Bucky from time to time, including Hulk sidekick **Rick Jones** and the young girl **Rikki Barnes** from the **Heroes Reborn** alternate universe. But the original character stayed mouldering in his grave.

BUCKY'S RETURN

But co-creator Jack Kirby expressed a desire that the original Bucky would return one day. And when **Ed Brubaker** took over writing the book, that was his plan too. Slowly over a number of years, in the volume you're reading now, he introduced the

character of **The Winter Soldier**, a Soviet cyborg creation, formed from the recovered, frozen body of Bucky, missing an arm. Cybernetics made up for the superpowers he never had. Used as a remote control assassin of the Soviet state through the 1960s, he was finally identified by **Sharon Carter**, long time friend of Captain America, as the original Bucky. Somehow Cap must find a way to come to terms with the fact that his former ally, seventy years out of time, is now an emotionless killing machine.

Currently, Ed Brubaker is telling the story of a young Bucky and how he came to be Captain America's sidekick back in the 40s. And telling a far darker story than Bucky's bright blue and red costume may have ever hinted at...

FURTHER READING

If you've enjoyed the style and art in this graphic novel, you may be interested in exploring some of these books too.

Captain America: The New Deal
Volume 27 of the Ultimate Marvel Graphic Novels Collection

At the book shop:
ISBN: 9780785149644

Captain America: Reborn

At the book shop:
ISBN:9781846534409

Fallen Son: Death of Captain America
Volume 51 of the Ultimate Marvel Graphic Novels Collection
At the book shop:
ISBN: 9780785128427

Marvel Platinum: The Definitive Captain America

At the book shop:
ISBN: 9781846534836

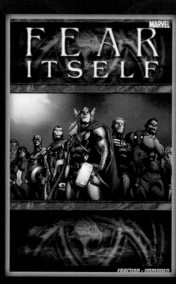

Fear Itself

At the book shop:
ISBN: 9781846534942

The Marvels Project

At the book shop:
ISBN: 978 0785140610